This book belongs to:

_____

Published by Yellow Button Press. ISBN: 9781692286859

MR. SQUIRREL
Is A Good Neighbor

Spreading Kindness

MaryLou Quillen

The Autumn winds are blowing
So you'll be seeing more of me
That's when acorn nuts start falling
From oak trees with golden leaves

I live in Jake's big backyard

In one of those golden trees

Jake watches as I gather nuts

And says 'Hello' to me

This story starts one September day

With a party for my friend, Jake

The neighborhood kids brought presents

And his mom made a birthday cake

Suddenly leaves started swirling

As the wind was whipping fast

Everyone ran for cover

And hoped this storm would pass

All the kiddos at the party

Left the yard in such a rush

Things were blowing to the ground

Then the breeze turned to a hush

I waited, watched, and waited

It looked like the kids had left for good

I thought, "I'll do something nice for Jake,

And the kids in our neighborhood!"

I looked around and noticed
presents were lying everywhere
Beautiful packages with shiny bows
Just scattered here and there

I did what a good neighbor would do
While juggling presents in the air
I worked to get them organized
and stacked them neatly by a chair

Balloons make parties happy
But the balloons were floating away
I dashed and scurried to gather them
And proudly put them on display

Next, I rescued the party bags
Blowing all around Jake's yard
I had to use my turbo boost
because chasing bags is hard

When I was finally finished
I looked around the yard to see
The kids had come back to the party
And they were cheering just for ME!

They jumped and cheered and smiled
"Yay, Mr. Squirrel has saved the day!"
They made ME the guest of honor
And invited me to stay!

Then they served me special treats
Like a nutty ice cream cone
Plus a slice of birthday cake
For me to eat at home

I found my simple act of kindness
Had given ME the gift of joy
I was glad to bring such happiness
To all those girls and boys

I know a SECRET about kindness
Here's a clue I'll share with you
Kind deeds can make others happy
And they will make YOU happy too!

Now I'm telling you my story
So you will look for ways to try
To spread some love and kindness
To friends and neighbors in YOUR life!

Interactive Questions

What is an "act of kindness"?

How does kindness make others feel?

How does kindness make you feel?

How did Mr. Squirrell show kindness?

How did the children show kindness?

What can you do to show kindness:

- 🌰 At school?

- 🌰 At the playground?

- 🌰 At home?

Plan 3 acts of kindness that you can do this week.

**If you enjoyed this book, please leave a review
on Amazon or Goodreads. Thank you!**

Made in the USA
Monee, IL
11 January 2023